Who Needs Glasses?

by Fran Manushkin

illustrated by Tammie Lyon

Katie Woo is published by Picture Window Books,
1710 Roe Crest Drive
North Mankato, Minnesota 56003
www.capstonepub.com

Library of Congress Cataloging-in-Publication Data
Manushkin, Fran.
Who needs glasses? / by Fran Manushkin; illustrated by Tammie Lyon.
p. cm. — (Katie Woo)
Summary: When Pedro keeps "losing" his eyeglasses, Katie shows him why it is alright—and necessary—to wear them.
ISBN 978-1-4048-7655-2 (library binding)
ISBN 978-1-4048-8049-8 (pbk.)
1. Woo, Katie (Fictitious character)—Juvenile fiction. 2. Chinese Americans—Juvenile fiction. 3. Eyeglasses—Juvenile fiction. 4. Pride and vanity—Juvenile fiction. 5. Elementary schools—Juvenile fiction. [1. Chinese American—Fiction. 2. Eyeglasses—Fiction. 3. Pride and vanity—Fiction. 4. Elementary schools—Fiction. 5. Schools—Fiction.] I. Lyon, Tammie, ill. II. Title. III. Series: Manushkin, Fran. Katie Woo.
PZ7.M3195Who 2013
813.54—dc23 2012029147

Art Director: Kay Fraser
Graphic Designer: Kristi Carlson

Photo Credits:
Greg Holch, pg. 26
Tammie Lyon, pg. 26

Printed in the United States of America in Stevens Point, Wisconsin.

092012
006937WZS13

Table of Contents

Chapter 1
Dinosaurs

"Today's class is about dinosaurs," said Miss Winkle. "This dinosaur is called Sue. It was named after the lady who found the bones."

"Cool!" said Katie.

Miss Winkle asked Pedro to read to the class. "I can't," he said. "My book is blurry."

"It's not," said Miss Winkle. "I think you need to get your eyes checked."

A few days later, Pedro showed Katie his new glasses.

"I feel a little weird," said Pedro.

"You look great!" said Katie.

"Today," said Miss Winkle, "we are making dinosaur dioramas. You will work in teams of three."

Chapter 2

Glasses Gone Missing

"Let's be a team," Katie told Pedro and JoJo. They began to work.

"Where are your glasses?" Katie asked Pedro.

"Um . . . I think I lost them," Pedro said.

Pedro began to read from his book. “Most dinosaurs ate pants.”

“No!” said Katie, laughing. “Not pants — plants!”

"Oh! Right!" said Pedro.

Pedro read another dinosaur fact: "The word 'dinosaur' means terrible blizzard."

"No!" Katie told him. "It's terrible lizard!"

"I'd better read the facts," Katie told Pedro. "You can start making our diorama."

"Great!" Pedro said. "I love to draw!"

Pedro drew a dinosaur.

"That looks like my cat," said Barry, the new boy.

Pedro squinted at his drawing. Katie told him, "I wish you could find your glasses."

During recess, Katie got an idea. She came back to class without her glasses.

"Where are they?" asked Pedro.

"I don't know," said Katie. "But I don't really need them."

Katie sat down.

"Watch out!" warned JoJo. "You are sitting on the clay for our diorama."

"Oops!" said Katie. "I didn't see that."

"I can make a paper dinosaur," said Katie. She squinted as she folded the paper.

"That looks like a boat," said Barry.

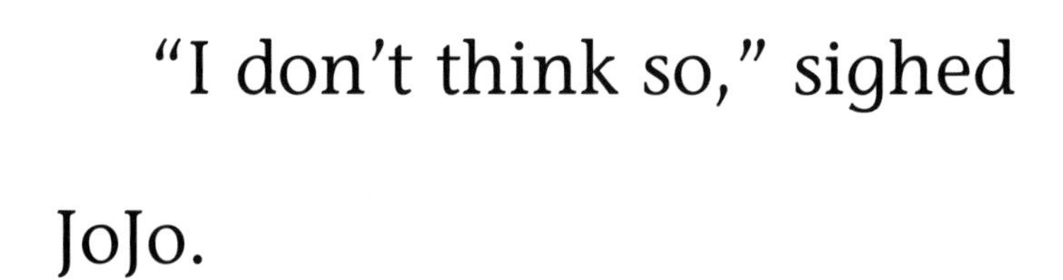

"Your team is very funny!"

"I don't think so," sighed JoJo.

Chapter 3

Project Saved!

"Our project is a mess!" said Katie. "And we are running out of time. If only I could find my glasses, then I could see!"

“Look!” said Pedro suddenly. “I found mine! They were in my pocket the whole time!”

Pedro began to work. He made a terrific clay dinosaur, and he painted a scary volcano.

"Looking good!" cheered Katie and JoJo.

"Very good!" agreed Barry.

"Hey!" said Katie. "Guess what? I found my glasses, too. They were in my pocket the whole time, too!"

Pedro laughed. “Katie, you are very tricky!”

“Maybe,” said Katie. She laughed too.

JoJo told Pedro, “You look smart in your glasses.”

“I feel smart,” he said, admiring his work.

Miss Winkle admired it too.

She took photos of all the teams and their projects.

Katie and Pedro and JoJo smiled proudly.

"You look terrific!" Miss Winkle said.

And they did!

About the Author

Fran Manushkin is the author of many popular picture books, including *Baby, Come Out!; Latkes and Applesauce: A Hanukkah Story; The Tushy Book; The Belly Book;* and *Big Girl Panties.* There is a real Katie Woo — she's Fran's great-niece — but she never gets in half the trouble of the Katie Woo in the books. Fran writes on her beloved Mac computer in New York City, without the help of her two naughty cats, Chaim and Goldy.

About the Illustrator

Tammie Lyon began her love for drawing at a young age while sitting at the kitchen table with her dad. She continued her love of art and eventually attended the Columbus College of Art and Design, where she earned a bachelors degree in fine art. After a brief career as a professional ballet dancer, she decided to devote herself full time to illustration. Today she lives with her husband, Lee, in Cincinnati, Ohio. Her dogs, Gus and Dudley, keep her company as she works in her studio.

Glossary

admiring (ad-MIRE-ing)—looking at something and enjoying it

blizzard (BLIZ-urd)—a heavy snowstorm

blurry (BLUR-ee)—smeared and unclear

diorama (dye-uh-RAM-uh)—a model of a scene made by placing figurines and other objects in front of a painted background

projects (PROJ-ekts)—school assignments that are worked on over a period of time

squinted (SKWINT-ed)—nearly closed eyes in order to see more clearly

terrific (tuh-RIF-ik)—very good or excellent

volcano (vol-KAY-noh)—a mountain with vents through which molten lava, ash, cinders, and gas erupt

Discussion Questions

1. Have you ever worked on a project with partners? Did you like it? Why or why not?

2. Why do you think Pedro did not want to wear his glasses?

3. Why are glasses important? What examples in the story explain why glasses are important?

Writing Prompts

1. Pretend you are picking out glasses. Write a paragraph to describe what the perfect pair of glasses look like. What color are they? What about shape?

2. Make a sign that talks about how great glasses are. Be sure to include a picture.

3. Katie's class was learning about dinosaurs. List three facts about dinosaurs. If you can't think of three, ask a grown-up to help you find some in a book or on the computer.

Having Fun with Katie Woo!

Glamour Glasses

Katie Woo loves her blue glasses. They are stylish, and best of all, they help her see. You can make your own glasses using pipe cleaners. They won't change how you see, but they will give you a new look for some fashion fun!

What you need:

- 4 pipe cleaners
- ruler
- scissors
- a variety of small jewels, poms, or other decorations
- glue

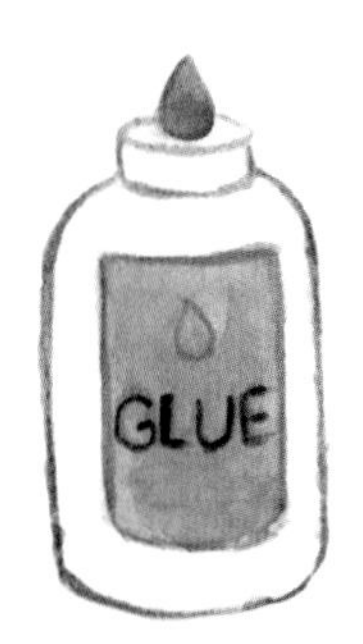

What you do:

1. Using the ruler to measure, cut two pipe cleaners so they are 8 inches long.

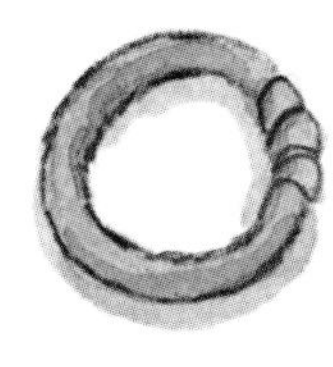

2. Take one of the 8-inch pipe cleaners and form it into the shape of your choice. You could make a circle, heart, or square. Repeat with the other 8-inch pipe cleaner. These are the "lenses."
3. Take a third pipe cleaner and fold it in half. Twist the two halves together.
4. Use the twisted pipe cleaner to connect your "lenses." For best results wrap each end around the lenses 3-4 times.
5. Cut the last pipe cleaner in half. Twist each piece around the lense section to make the bows of the frame. Add a curve at the ends so the glasses fit around your ears.
6. Now you can decorate your glasses! Attach jewels, poms, or other small decorations with glue. Let dry.

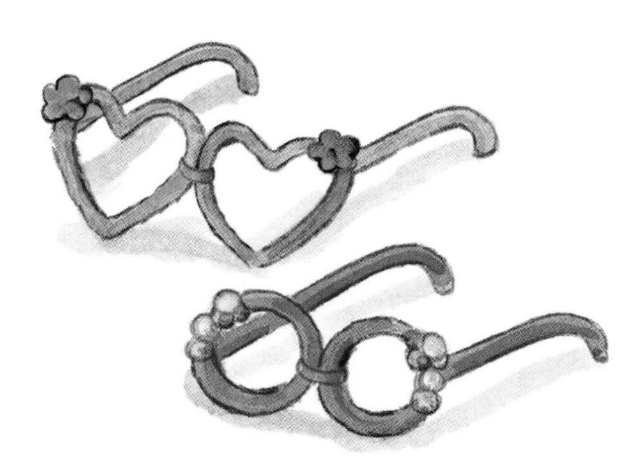

THE FUN DOESN'T
STOP HERE!

Discover more at www.capstonekids.com
Videos & Contests
Games & Puzzles
Friends & Favorites
Authors & Illustrators
Find cool websites and more books like this one at www.facthound.com. Just type in the Book ID: 9781404876552 and you're ready to go!